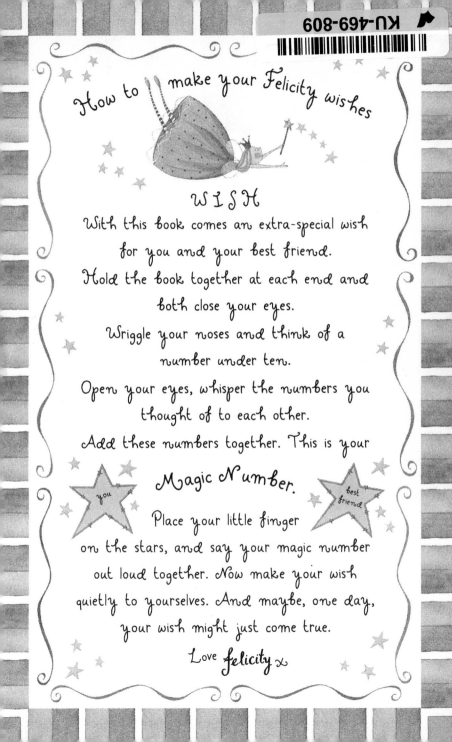

How to make your Felicity wishes

WISH

With this book comes an extra-special wish
for you and your best friend.

Hold the book together at each end and
both close your eyes.

Wriggle your noses and think of a
number under ten.

Open your eyes, whisper the numbers you
thought of to each other.

Add these numbers together. This is your

Magic Number.

you

best friend

Place your little finger
on the stars, and say your magic number
out loud together. Now make your wish
quietly to yourselves. And maybe, one day,
your wish might just come true.

Love felicity x

For Taz, Natasha, Ella and Josh. x

FELICITY WISHES

Felicity Wishes © 2000 Emma Thomson
Licensed by White Lion Publishing

Text and Illustrations © 2007 Emma Thomson

First published in Great Britain in 2007 by Hodder Children's Books

A Catalogue record for this book is available from the British Library.

ISBN: 9 780 34094396 0

Printed in the UK by CPI Bookmarque, Croydon, CR0 4TD

The paper and board used in this paperback by Hodder Children's Books are natural recyclable
products made from wood grown in sustainable forests. The manufacturing processes
conform to the environmental regulations of the country of origin.

Hodder Children's Books
A division of Hachette Children's Books, 338 Euston Road, London NW1 3BH

CONTENTS

Tasty Trip

Felicity Wishes was very excited – she and her friends were off on holiday together! They were sitting in Sparkles, their favourite café, trying to decide where to go.

"I think we should go on a hiking holiday to Lotolakes!" Winnie said, fluttering enthusiastically. "It's not very far from here, and I've always wanted to go."

"But why there?" asked Holly. "Why not Bubble Island or Petal Mountain?"

"Because I've been to Bubble Island and we've all been to Petal Mountain, and Lotolakes sounds like the perfect place to go hiking," Winnie replied.

"It does sound a bit boring," complained Holly.

"It may sound boring, but it's the only place in Fairy World where you can get..." Winnie paused dramatically, "Lotolakes chocolate!"

"Oh, I've heard of that!" said Felicity, suddenly jumping up. "It's supposed to be the tastiest chocolate ever made!"

"If it's that good, why can't you get it here?" Holly asked sceptically.

"Because it doesn't travel well. Apparently, anywhere outside of Lotolakes it tastes disgusting!" Felicity replied.

"So why don't they make it here?" Daisy asked.

"The recipe is a very well-kept

secret. No one knows how to make it," Winnie informed her.

"Well, if I get to taste yummy chocolate and have an adventure in the wide outdoors, I'm happy!" said Daisy, smiling.

The fairies all agreed, and flew home to pack.

* * *

The next morning they met bright and early, complete with bulging backpacks and brand-new walking shoes.

The journey to Lotolakes wasn't very long. First the fairies had to get a bus from Little Blossoming to Bloomfield – they couldn't fly very far because of their heavy bags. Then they had to get a train to Misty Glen and finally another bus to Lotolakes.

"It's not far to the campsite, according to my map!" called Winnie, leading the way as they stepped off the bus.

The scenery was breathtaking.
The bus had stopped by the side of
a road in what looked like the middle
of nowhere. There were no houses or
shops in sight, only miles and miles
of tall dark trees, overlooked by rolling
green hills. By the side of the road
was a trickling stream, running with
the clearest water any of the fairies
had ever seen.

"How far exactly is the campsite,
Winnie?" asked Holly.

Felicity looked around. There were
no other fairies in sight.

"We have to follow this footpath,"

said Winnie, pointing to a muddy path winding through the next field, "then we go over a wall, through another field, round a lake, past a meadow and over a bridge. There are no roads to the campsite, so it should be nice and quiet there!"

The fairies looked at Winnie in wonder. Apart from the gentle trickling of the stream, they couldn't hear anything – or imagine anywhere quieter.

"Come on then!" called Winnie, charging over the stream and along the footpath, the other fairies following more slowly.

The friends fluttered the first part of the way, but their wings soon became tired under their heavy loads, so they all resorted to walking – except for Winnie, who was used to this kind of adventure.

"My brand-new pink boots are getting muddy!" Felicity moaned as she delicately manoeuvred a puddle. "I really hope my new dress doesn't too."

The words were no sooner out of her mouth when Felicity slipped and toppled backwards into a very muddy puddle!

"Oh no, Felicity!" Daisy ran up to her

and held out her hand to help Felicity up, only to slip over!

Holly, Polly and Winnie tried to help their friends, but they were also trying very hard not to slip over as well. Before long they were all in fits of giggles, slipping and sliding around in the mud.

"I'd love to take a picture of us now!" Holly said. "No one at school will ever believe I got mud in my hair!"

Eventually the fairies managed to get up and keep walking. But before long they were exhausted.

"How much further, Winnie?" Daisy asked droopily.

"Not far!" Winnie replied. But she'd said exactly the same thing the last time she was asked!

Finally they reached the campsite. Felicity, Polly, Holly and Daisy immediately unfastened the heavy bags from their backs and dropped them to the ground, falling on top of them in a big heap. There were a few other fairies setting up their tents, and they smiled sympathetically.

"I've-never-walked-that-far!" Holly said, panting.

"My feet hurt!" Felicity moaned. "Why didn't I get the sensible walking shoes Winnie recommended?"

Daisy's wings were almost touching the ground, they were drooping so much!

Just then Winnie came back from the campsite shop, holding five large chocolate bars.

"These are for you-hoo," she sang energetically.

"I'm too tired to eat," Polly said, closing her eyes.

"Trust me, you want to eat these!" Winnie said, handing one to each fairy.

They peeled the wrappers back and started nibbling their bars of chocolate.

Almost at once the fairies cheered up.

"Thish ish elishoush," Felicity said, her mouth full.

"I heel besher aleady," Holly announced as she chewed.

They finished the chocolate with incredible speed and all jumped up from the ground, full of energy.

Winnie grinned. "I told you it was the best chocolate in Fairy World!"

But Daisy didn't hear; she was too busy examining the small picture on the wrapper. "It's a bellapop flower," she whispered.

"What's a bellapop flower?" Felicity asked, looking at the logo on her own wrapper.

"I thought it had been forgotten about centuries ago," Daisy said dreamily. "Supposedly it used to grow in the most magical places in Fairy World – but none has been reported for years, and I thought they were extinct."

"Why would they use a flower no one has ever heard of for their logo?" Holly asked.

"That's what I'm wondering," Daisy said, a thoughtful look on her face.

"Well, come on, everyone! We have to get our tents up before dark," Winnie said.

They found the perfect spot, with a wonderful view, and as soon as they'd set up the tents, each fairy climbed into her sleeping bag, ready for a good night's sleep.

✳ ✳ ✳

The next morning Winnie woke everyone very early.

"Time for our first hike!" she announced, unzipping Felicity and Polly's tent.

"We had that yesterday," Felicity groaned from under the cover of her sleeping bag.

"That wasn't a hike! That was a short walk!" Winnie said cheerfully.

Felicity, who had never been a morning fairy, rolled over and pulled her pillow over her head.

Winnie pulled it off and threw it towards Polly!

"Pillow fight!" Felicity squealed, and Holly and Daisy rushed in to join them.

Quite some time later the fairies emerged from the tent, fluffy-haired and dishevelled, and all wide awake, ready to begin their hike.

* * *

Once again it wasn't long before Felicity, Holly, Polly and Daisy were worn out.

"Are we actually going somewhere?" Polly asked Winnie.

"The purpose of a hike is not to reach a destination, merely to enjoy the walking," Winnie said, fluttering ahead again.

"Or flying!" Daisy called out from behind.

"But what's the point, if you're not going anywhere?" Holly asked.

"You never know what you might find along the way!" Winnie called.

But the fairies began to dawdle. Felicity picked up a stick and started drawing pictures in the mud. Holly

took out her
hairbrush from her
bag and restyled her
hair. Polly sat down and began to
read her book and Daisy took
out her magnifying glass to
have a closer look at
the plant life.

"OK, maybe it is
time for a break,"
said Winnie reluctantly.
"But only five minutes."

"Can't we just go back to the
campsite?" Polly asked hopefully.

"If only we had some more
chocolate," said Daisy dreamily.

"Ta da!" Winnie pulled five bars of

chocolate from her bag and gave one to each fairy. "I was saving them until you were all completely worn out," she said, "and now seems like a good time!"

"It does look good," said Polly, "but think about your teeth! Maybe one little bite wouldn't hurt, though…" she murmured as she unwrapped a bar.

The fairies devoured their chocolate bars in seconds and immediately perked up.

"Time to get moving!" said Felicity, jumping up. "You don't have any more of that chocolate, by any chance, Winnie?"

But Winnie was unfolding her map worriedly, and turning it in every direction.

"What's wrong?" Felicity asked.

"I think we're lost," Winnie replied bluntly.

"We can't be. Look, we came on that

path there…" Holly realized that there were three paths leading to the small clearing they had been sitting in.

"Where were we when you last looked at the map, Winnie?" Polly asked sensibly.

"At the campsite," Winnie replied.

The fairies all stood in silence, Winnie studying her compass.

"I think we should take that path." She pointed.

The fairies all followed her, unable to think of anything better to do.

After a few minutes they fluttered out of the woods and came to the edge of a large field, the start of some rolling green hills. Winnie took out her binoculars and began looking around her.

"Wow!" she said in surprise.

"What is it?" Daisy asked, squinting into the distance.

But Winnie was already off, fluttering across the field at top speed. They hurried after her – and there in the side of the hill was the opening to a cave!

Something had caught Daisy's eye and she was kneeling on the ground, just by the cave opening.

"I don't believe it," she whispered.

Felicity bent down beside her. Daisy was gently stroking the fragile petals of a flower.

"That's pretty," Felicity remarked.

"It's not just pretty," Daisy replied, "it's magical!"

Felicity looked at her quizzically.

"It's a bellapop flower!" Daisy explained.

"The one from the chocolate wrapper?" Polly asked, kneeling down as well.

"Yes. It only grows in the most magical places in Fairy World," Daisy reminded her friends.

"Well, that makes me want to go into the cave even more!" said Winnie in delight.

"Oh no, you won't catch me going in there!" said Holly, wrinkling her nose. "It's all damp and dark, and my hair will go frizzy!"

"Come on, Hol, we've got to have a look!" called Felicity.

"We'll come out if there's nothing to see," Polly reasoned.

Winnie took Holly's hand and led the way, shining her torch into the darkness.

"Yoo-hoo!" she called into the cave. The sound bounced off the walls, echoing all around her.

"Hellllooooooo," Felicity called, giggling.

The fairies walked further and further in, making silly sounds as they went.

"Hang on a minute," Winnie said,

coming to a halt. Felicity, Holly, Polly and Daisy stopped behind her.

"There's a light ahead," Winnie whispered. She continued walking until they came to a very large candle, fixed to the cave wall.

"And there's another!" said Winnie, rushing ahead.

The fairies followed the lights until they came to a huge cavern with a very large, very dark lake in its centre.

"Chocolate!" Felicity blurted out loudly.

"No, I haven't got any more, sorry," Winnie reminded her.

"No, chocolate," Felicity said again, pointing at the lake. She'd walked to the very edge and, as her friends watched in wonder, she kept walking until her feet, then her legs and her skirt were immersed in the lake.

"Felicity, come back, you're getting soaked!" Daisy shouted, rushing forward.

"Your dress will get ruined!" Holly warned.

But still Felicity continued.

"Your hair!" Polly screeched.

By now Felicity was taking huge gulps of the lake, pushing it into her open mouth with her hands. "Iss shockert!" she called back to her friends.

Winnie dipped her foot in the lake. Her boot came out covered in dark-brown liquid.

"It *is* chocolate!" said Daisy, amazed.

The fairies looked back up again, only to find that Felicity had completely disappeared.

"Where's she gone?" Holly shrieked.

Winnie began to wade in to look for Felicity, diving underneath the surface. Holly, Polly and Daisy watched, waiting for Winnie to emerge… but she didn't!

"Quick, hold hands, we'll all go in

together," Polly said, taking Holly's and Daisy's hands and leading them into the lake. They ducked their heads under the surface, but couldn't see anything in the thick brown chocolate. The further they went the thicker it got and Polly, holding her friends' hands, pulled them as far as she dared go – then there was a blinding light, and everything disappeared!

* * *

When the fairy friends came to their senses again, they were no longer covered in chocolate, and the lake had disappeared entirely!

"Where are we?" Felicity wondered aloud as she looked around her. It was a bright, sunny afternoon in the countryside – but something wasn't quite right. Suddenly Felicity realized what it was: everything she could see, grass, flowers, stones, trees, was made of chocolate!

"It's wonderful!" said Holly, chewing on a buttercup.

"It's magical!" Daisy grinned. This magical place was why the bellapop flowers were able to grow!

"Now we know where Lotolakes chocolate comes from!" said Felicity, gathering a handful of chocolate pebbles. "And we can eat as much of it as we want!"

The fairies felt as though they had fallen into a dreamland. But as each of them began to nibble the chocolate plants around them, they realized that nothing in a dream could taste as good!

Sometimes life
can be as yummy

as a chocolate-filled dream!

Chocolate Chaos

Felicity Wishes and her friends Holly, Polly, Winnie and Daisy were on a very magical holiday! They'd discovered a magical cave with a chocolate lake inside, leading to a whole world made of chocolate!

"How did we get here?" Felicity asked, relaxing on the dark chocolate grass.

"I don't know, but it's wonderful!" Holly cried, doing a loop-the-loop in the air as she chewed on a chocolate leaf from a nearby tree.

Everything the fairies could see was

made of chocolate – the yummiest, most delicious chocolate any of them had ever tasted. It was Lotolakes chocolate – unavailable anywhere else in Fairy World. The recipe had been a closely guarded secret for many years.

As Felicity and her friends watched, white chocolate petals danced on chocolate flowers, dark chocolate tree trunks waved in the gentle breeze and chocolate leaves rustled over their heads!

"I hope we can stay here for ever," said Daisy happily. Just then, she spotted something move behind a nearby bush.

"What was that?" she called to her friends, who were playing chase around a large tree.

Felicity rushed up and tapped Daisy on the shoulder.

"You're it!" she shouted, zooming away. Forgetting about what she'd seen,

Daisy joined in with the game. But ten minutes later she stopped short. "There, I saw it again!" she called to her friends, sure this time she had seen a tiny wing fluttering behind the same bush.

"Is anyone in there?" Winnie called excitedly, fluttering up to the bush. "Come out, come out, whoever you are!"

All at once a swarm of tiny fairies came darting out from the very middle of the bush. They formed a tight circle around Felicity, Polly, Winnie, Daisy and Holly, who all found it rather funny and started to laugh.

"Names!" one of the tiny fairies demanded in a high-pitched squeaky voice, looking directly at Felicity.

"Felicity Wishes," she replied boldly. "And this is Holly—"

The tiny fairy interrupted her. "State the purpose of your visit," it squeaked.

"To eat as much chocolate as possible," cut in Holly, in fits of giggles.

The tiny fairies all looked very cross.

"Come with us," one of them squeaked, before they started to fly across the field. Felicity and her friends felt they had no choice but to follow.

✳ ✳ ✳

"I'm not sure I like this," said Daisy worriedly as the fairies flew along the river's edge.

"It's an adventure!" replied Winnie, who always loved excitement.

Soon the fairies came to a huge chocolate lake, with the most amazing castle standing upon an island in the middle of it.

The castle was an assortment of turrets, windows and doors, all thrown

together in a jumble. A large flag was flying from the tallest turret in the middle, waving a picture of the bellapop flower, the most magical flower in Fairy World.

"Wow," Felicity mouthed, too shocked to speak out loud.

The castle glistened and glinted in the sunshine, its chocolate bricks sparkling like fairy lights. The tiny fairies led Felicity and her friends on to a bridge that crossed the lake, and entered the grand castle.

"Why doesn't it melt?" Felicity wondered aloud, looking up at the vast entrance hall. The ceiling was very high, a glass dome at the top flooding the room with sunlight. Fires were alight in chocolate grates on both sides of the hall and several very comfortable-looking armchairs dotted the floor.

The tiny fairies had disappeared up a grand staircase in the centre of the entrance hall, only to reappear seconds later.

"Follow us!" they demanded.

Felicity, Winnie, Holly, Polly and Daisy did as they were told, following the fairies straight up the staircase and into another large room at the top of the stairs.

The tiny fairies parted in front of them, to reveal a normal-size fairy sitting in a very beautiful chair at the end of the room, a chocolate crown glinting upon her head.

"Gosh!" blurted Felicity, staring in wonder at the queen ahead of her.

"Gosh indeed!" said the queen. "That's what I thought when I heard there were intruders in my land."

"We didn't mean to intrude!" Felicity began immediately. "It was an accident! We didn't know the chocolate lake would lead to a chocolate land."

"Hmm. And what did you do once you discovered where you were?" asked the queen, looking at the five fairies in turn. "Did you try to go back to where you came from?"

"No," replied Felicity, feeling slightly ashamed.

"We were having too much fun to go back!" said Holly boldly. "We love it here!"

The tiny fairies, standing either side of Felicity and her friends, all began to speak at once, their squeaky voices becoming deafening in the large room.

"This is not a place to have fun!" one of the little fairies shouted.

"Make them work!" Holly heard another yell.

"They can't go back, you know the law!" Felicity heard. She grabbed hold of Winnie's arm.

"What if they don't let us go home?" she asked Winnie. "It has been fun, but I don't want to stay here for ever. What about all our friends at home in Little Blossoming?"

A hush immediately fell upon the room as the queen stood up.

"I shall consider how to deal with you. Remain here until I return," she said, walking towards the door.

The tiny fairies followed her, resuming their shouts. The door shut behind them and Felicity could hear the sound of a key turning in the lock.

The fairy friends were alone.

"We're captives!" Daisy squealed, her voice almost as highly pitched as the tiny fairies'.

"Don't be silly. She can see we're only novice fairies," Polly reasoned.

"But it's the law that they can't let us go!" said Felicity, becoming more and more worried.

"That's fine by me!" grinned Holly. "Chocolate for breakfast, lunch and supper, all day, every day!"

Winnie knew they needed an escape plan. There must be some way to get out of the castle! She fluttered around the room – but all the windows and doors were locked.

Just then, Felicity had a brainwave.

"I've got a plan!" she squeaked. "All we have to do is… eat our way out of the castle!"

Polly stared at her. "But the walls are really thick – think what all the chocolate would do to our teeth!"

"We can brush our teeth as soon as we get home," Winnie reassured her. "I think it's a great plan – let's get going!"

The fairies flew round the room, trying to find the thinnest piece of wall. But they'd eaten a lot of chocolate already that day, and one by one they flew back down to the floor, feeling unwell.

"I'm not sure I can bear another bite!" said Felicity pathetically. "I usually love chocolate, and I'm sure I will again – but I've eaten more chocolate today than I've ever had before!"

"I feel the same," groaned Holly.

Just then, there was a noise at the door and the queen came marching back into the room.

"The law is very clear on how to proceed in this situation," she began. "The way to this land has been discovered by you. It is a closely guarded secret and I cannot allow you to reveal it."

Felicity, Winnie, Holly, Polly and Daisy stared at her in shock.

"So you really are going to keep us here?" asked Felicity.

"I have no choice," the queen replied.

"Of course you have a choice. You're the queen!" exclaimed Winnie.

"I'm afraid it's not as simple as that," the queen said sadly, taking a chair next to the fairies. "I have to consider the wishes of my people."

"Can't we offer you something in return for our release?" suggested Polly.

"We could tell everyone in Fairy World how good Lotolakes chocolate is!" said Felicity excitedly. "We could even set up a shop for you in Little

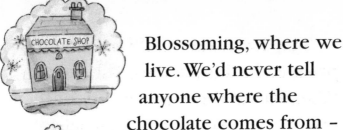

Blossoming, where we live. We'd never tell anyone where the chocolate comes from – and we never break our promises!" she said, smiling warmly at the queen.

The fairies held their breath. None of them really wanted to stay there for ever – they would all miss their homes and their normal lives at school.

The queen sat for a few seconds, deep in thought, then she jumped up and fluttered out of the door, where the tiny fairies were waiting. Felicity and her friends could hear a whispered conversation going on, but couldn't work out what was being said, no matter how hard they tried.

But when the queen came back, her face was covered in a huge smile.

"My people agree with me that this is a wonderful idea! We will make arrangements for the delivery of the chocolate – and you are free to go!"

The fairies danced around the room for joy, and Felicity couldn't resist giving the queen a huge hug. But Polly was looking thoughtful.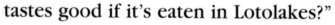

"There's only one thing," she said reluctantly. "Isn't it true that Lotolakes chocolate only tastes good if it's eaten in Lotolakes?"

"Oh, don't worry about that!" reassured the queen. "We normally add a special ingredient to the mixture which means it doesn't taste good outside Lotolakes. But we will take that ingredient out of the chocolate we supply to you. That way, you'll be able to sell it to fairies all over Little Blossoming!"

The fairies cheered. Felicity was already thinking about how she would decorate their new chocolate shop, and Polly was wondering where they should open it.

"Let me show you where the chocolates are made," the queen said, leading Felicity and her friends out of the room, and up a steep staircase. At the very top, she opened a door into an enormous workshop situated right on top of the castle, with windows looking out in every direction. It was beautiful.

"As you can see, our fairies here work very hard to produce our chocolate. Every ingredient must be added in the correct order and in the correct quantity, or disastrous consequences will occur," the queen told them. "Once they are made, we ensure that each chocolate is beautifully packaged in a glittering bag."

The fairies looked round the room in wonder. The room was filled with humming machines and tiny buzzing fairies.

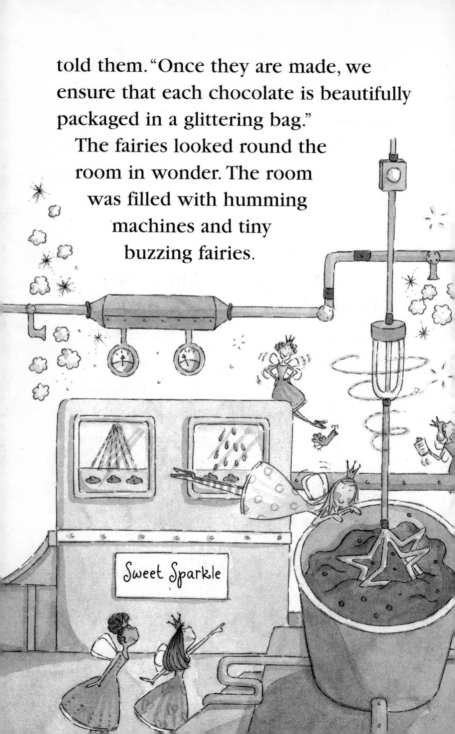

Sweet Sparkle

Felicity fluttered up to the rim of one large metal drum, to see a huge star-shaped whisk busily stirring the liquid chocolate inside.

STRAWBERRY SURPRISE

LEMONY SHERBERT

CHERRY FIZZ

"How many different kinds of chocolates do you make?" Daisy asked the queen.

"Around three hundred and forty-two – but new ones are invented all the time."

Felicity was amazed. These tiny fairies knew how to make over three hundred different chocolates, and she knew she would struggle to remember even one.

"This is definitely my favourite," said the queen, stopping beside a machine made all of glass. It was rotating upside down and round and round, the pink mixture inside becoming more and more fluffy as it was tumbled about.

"Strawberry surprise!" said the queen proudly. "The lightest, most delicious strawberry filling you will ever taste."

At that moment a tiny fairy arrived, holding a tray of six small chocolates in the shape of whole strawberries.

"Thank you, Annie," the queen said, taking the tray and offering it to Felicity and her friends.

They each took one and bit into the hard chocolate shell.

The queen had been right! The strawberry filling was so light it was almost floating out of the half-eaten chocolate still held in their hands, and as they ate it filled their mouths, noses and ears with a sweet strawberry flavour, so delicious they immediately wanted more.

But the queen had started to move again, continuing to show them around the factory.

Each new discovery was more amazing than the last, but finally the tour was over. Felicity and her friends were exhausted but happy. Not only had they had an amazing adventure, but another adventure was on its way – they were going to open their very own chocolate shop, every fairy's dream!

Wherever you are and whatever you are doing

there may be adventure just around the corner!

Glittering Giveaways

Felicity Wishes and her friends Holly, Daisy, Winnie and Polly were in a land where everything was made out of chocolate! The queen of the land was showing them the workshop where chocolates were made, and the fairies were trying desperately to remember at least some of them. When they'd finished their tour, the queen gave them dozens of glittering bags filled with chocolates to take back to Little Blossoming.

Felicity and her friends wanted to return to Little Blossoming immediately. They were going to open their very own chocolate shop!

"Goodbye! Goodbye!" cried the queen.

"Come and visit us soon!" said Felicity, hugging her tightly. She was glad to have made a new friend in this strange new land.

Then the queen waved her wand over the five fairies, there was a flash of brilliant light, and they found themselves back in the campsite! It was very strange to be back in a world where nothing was made out of chocolate, and it felt like they'd been away for a very long time.

* * *

The fairies slept the night at the campsite, then packed up their tents in the morning and started the hike back to the bus stop. Fortunately, they had lots of chocolate with them to give them energy for the long journey back to Little Blossoming!

* * *

"Let's start looking for a shop straight away!" said Holly excitedly as they got wearily off the bus.

"I think we should get some sleep first. Then we'll look first thing tomorrow morning," Polly suggested sensibly.

The fairies were all tired after their adventure and agreed that this was a good idea. Felicity fluttered home, delighted to be back in her own bed again. The second that her head hit her pillow she was fast asleep, dreaming of the fun they would all have in their very own chocolate shop.

* * *

The next day, they met in Sparkles to discuss their plans. Winnie was poring over Little Blossoming's local newspaper.

"What about that one?" Holly asked, pointing to a picture of a large shop in the advertisements column.

"No, it's too far away from the school so we'll miss the after-school rush for sweets," Polly said, looking at another picture. "This one is more sensible."

But Felicity didn't like the look of the shop Polly had chosen. It was just one large, square room, painted a boring white.

"No, we need something with more character," sighed Felicity. So far, none of the shops was what she had imagined.

Daisy turned the page – and the fairies all gasped.

"That's it!" squealed Felicity excitedly.

"It's beautiful," said Daisy.

The shop was purple, with pink and white striped window frames, just perfect for Felicity and her friends.

"Let's go!" Holly had already put her

coat on and was halfway out of the door.

The fairies quickly fluttered to Sweet Street, a small cobbled road tucked away behind Little Blossoming's high street. They peered through the glass front of the shop to see two rooms, divided by a large archway in the middle.

"We can have the counter and all the plain chocolates on one side, and the chocolates with fillings on the other." Daisy began, mapping out the shop in her mind.

"We can cover the wall at the back with a rich, sumptuous wallpaper, and the other walls can be painted to reflect the colours, but much plainer so that it doesn't feel too cluttered," said Holly, imagining the exact patterns she would choose.

Felicity knocked on the door. It was opened by a kindly-looking fairy in an apron.

"We've come to ask about the shop!" Felicity started. "We read that it might be available, and we'd love to take it on. We're opening a chocolate shop!"

"You've arrived at just the right time," said the fairy. "I ran this as a sweet shop for many years, but I've decided I want to give it up and travel round Fairy World in search of adventure. You seem like the perfect fairies to take over from me!"

Felicity jumped for joy. Her dream was coming true!

The kindly fairy showed them round the shop, telling them all about her years there. They explained all their plans. There was so much to be done before the shop opened! But they knew that if each fairy chose a specific task it shouldn't take too long.

* * *

Over the next two days Felicity, Winnie, Polly, Holly and Daisy spent all their time in the new shop.

Winnie constructed glass shelves to display the delicious chocolates. Daisy designed and made the gift boxes.

Holly chose the wallpaper and paint for the walls: a light-blue background with large chocolate-brown swirls on the back wall, and light blue on the side walls, with a horizontal brown line running along the middle. Polly organized the delivery of the chocolates and arranged them on the shelves when they arrived and Felicity designed posters advertising the shop's opening. She put them up all around Little Blossoming, and told every fairy she saw not to miss out on the grand opening day.

None of the fairies slept a wink the
night before the shop was due to
open, they were all so excited.

"Are all the chocolates in place?"
Felicity asked, carrying out a final
inspection of everything.

"Check!" Polly called from under
the counter.

"Are the gift boxes ready?" Felicity
continued, following her list.

"Check!" Daisy called from the
archway.

"Are the walls completely dry?"
Felicity asked.

"Check!" Holly called, relieved.

"Then
let's open!"

They had taped
white paper to the
windows so that no one
could see in. Winnie pulled
it down to reveal a queue of
fairies all jumping up and down
excitedly.

"Gosh!" squealed Daisy. "Your
advertising worked, Felicity!"

The queue of fairies was so long
that Felicity couldn't even see the
end of it! It stretched all the way
along the road and around the corner.

"How will they all fit in?" asked Felicity worriedly.

"Don't worry," Winnie said, rushing to the door.

The fairies all took their places: Holly and Daisy behind the counter; Polly and Felicity either side of the arch to help undecided fairies chose a chocolate that suited them; and Winnie by the door, only allowing a certain number of fairies in at a time and giving each one their free glittering bag with a chocolate inside.

The day passed very quickly – and just as Felicity could finally glimpse the end of the queue, it was nearly time to close.

"I'm sure some of those fairies came back twice!" said Holly, so exhausted she had to sit down on the counter. "I heard one fairy say she'd come in three times today and is going to come back first thing tomorrow!" said Daisy, leaning on one of the shelves.

"We've got a problem!" announced Polly. She was twirling around in the middle of the room, looking at the shelves.

As Felicity, Winnie, Daisy and Holly looked, they realized what the problem was. The shelves were completely empty.

"Haven't we got any more?" Felicity asked hopefully, even though she knew they had nowhere to store more chocolates.

"We put everything the queen sent on the shelves," replied Polly. "Except for the chocolate powder she sent for pure chocolate."

"What are we going to do?" wailed Daisy. "We can't open tomorrow without any chocolates!"

"There's only one thing we can do," said Felicity calmly. "We'll have to make some more."

The fairies all looked at her uncertainly.

"But the queen said that every ingredient had to be exact, or there would be disastrous consequences," Polly reminded them all.

"Then we will get everything exact! I'm sure we can remember together," said Winnie cheerfully.

So the fairies all went back to Felicity's house to begin making their own chocolates.

It took all night – and the kitchen

was a complete mess by the time they
had finished. There was chocolate
splattered up the walls, on the curtains,
all over the floor and even in the
cupboards! But the fairies had made
enough chocolates to fill the shelves
again. Felicity was desperate to taste
one, but they had all agreed that all
the chocolates they made should be
sold in the shop, to avoid running out.

* * *

When they arrived at the shop, loaded down with chocolates, there was already a long queue of fairies waiting outside. They rushed the chocolates out on to the shelves just in time for their opening at nine o'clock.

"Phew!" sighed Felicity as she opened the shop door. "I didn't think we'd make it on time."

For the first few hours the shop was very busy. Winnie had to stand at the door once again to control the number of fairies coming in.

But after a while the queue simply disappeared.

"I wonder where they all went," said Daisy, peering up and down the deserted street.

"I don't know about you, but all this hard work has made me hungry and we've got plenty of chocolates," replied Felicity, biting into a white chocolate cloud. "Mmm, we did well.

This is even better than the real thing!"

Then all at once something strange began to happen. As Felicity's friends watched her in disbelief, she began to float up towards the ceiling.

Her wings weren't even fluttering. Felicity, unaware, started to pick up a second white chocolate.

"No, don't!" screamed Polly, leaping up towards Felicity and knocking the chocolate out of her hand.

"Really, Polly, there are plenty left. It doesn't matter if I have just one more," said Felicity. But then she realized that she couldn't reach down to the counter. In fact, she was almost touching the ceiling!

"Don't worry, Felicity, we'll get you down!" cried Winnie, fluttering up to where Felicity was floating against the ceiling.

As Winnie dragged Felicity back to the floor, Polly was pointing speechlessly outside the shop. The queue of fairies had returned! But they looked very, very different.

The first fairy
in the queue had
sprigs of mint
growing out of her
head, the second
had gone the colour
of a strawberry from
the tips of her wings
to her toes,
and the
third was
upside
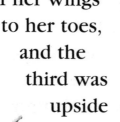
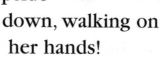
down, walking on
her hands!
The queue was just
as long as it had been
the day before, but
each fairy had changed
in some way according
to the chocolates she had eaten.

Daisy immediately shut the door to
the shouts and yells coming from the
fairies outside and dived behind the

counter where Felicity, Holly, Polly and Winnie were already hiding.

"What are we going to do?" Felicity asked, holding on to the leg of the counter to stop herself floating away.

"I don't know!" sobbed Holly.

There was a loud knock on the door.

Felicity peeped over the top of the counter to see the queen from Lotolakes standing outside. Looking past her, she saw that every fairy in the queue was back to normal.

Winnie dashed over to open the door and let the queen in.

"I came as soon as I heard. What happened?" she asked, looking at Felicity, who was holding on to Polly to keep her down.

"We ran out of chocolate so we had to make our own – we didn't want to disappoint anyone, but we didn't know this would happen!" Felicity replied, hanging her head.

The queen waved her wand and Felicity came down to the ground with a bump.

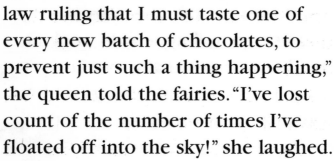

"A long time ago, I made a law ruling that I must taste one of every new batch of chocolates, to prevent just such a thing happening," the queen told the fairies. "I've lost count of the number of times I've floated off into the sky!" she laughed.

"We're really sorry," apologized Polly.

"You weren't to know. And you only wanted to do what was best," said the queen kindly.

Holly had been wondering how the queen had known about the disaster. "How did you find out so quickly?"

"Some of my fairies came to find out how you were getting on, and they immediately reported back to me," the queen explained.

"Will we have to close the shop?" asked Daisy sadly.

"No, don't worry about that! You've done a wonderful job setting the shop up and decorating it. But it's time for my fairies to move in and run it now. And that way we can make sure that there aren't any more chocolate disasters!"

Felicity, Holly, Polly, Winnie and Daisy immediately cheered up.

"You can come and work here during every holiday and at the weekends if you want," offered the queen. "The rest of the time you will always be our favourite customers!"

The fairies thanked the queen and started to take their chocolates off the shelves, replacing them with the new chocolates the queen had brought with her.

As they reopened the doors, Felicity and her friends assured their customers that these chocolate would not have

any hidden surprises! It wasn't long
before the shop was filled once again
with excited fairies.

Felicity looked round the buzzing shop, full of friends, and smelt the lovely chocolatey smell. She couldn't imagine a better place to be.

There's no better
place to be
than with your best friends.

Emma Thomson's
felicity Wishes

Felicity and her friends are

desperate to win a place on

the school newspaper in

Newspaper Nerves

Newspaper Nerves

Felicity Wishes flew with heavy wings towards school. It was Monday morning. Monday had become Felicity's least favourite day since the start of the new term. Each week began with an extra-long class of double Magic Maths.

"If only we could start the week with something more fun, like cooking," sighed Felicity as she led the way out of assembly with her friends Holly, Polly and Daisy.

"I can't understand why you don't

like it. Maths really is magic!" said
Polly, who was the cleverest of all the
fairy friends by far.

"There's only one thing magic about
maths, and that's how every minute in
the class feels like an hour!" giggled
Felicity, stopping to look at the school
noticeboard.

Felicity, Holly, Polly and Daisy all
went to the School of Nine Wishes.
One day they would graduate to
become proper fairies with a beautiful
pair of double wings.

"Hey! Look at this!" said Holly
pointing to a poster. "It may be just
the thing to help
you have a happy
Monday morning,
Felicity!"

* * *

Felicity was gone
in a flutter leaving
Polly, Daisy and

Nine Wishes
Newspaper

The School of Nine Wishes
announces the launch of
a School Newspaper.
VOLUNTEERS WANTED
Meet Monday
9.30 a.m. Room 10

Holly to go to Magic Maths without her. When she met up with them at break-time she could hardly contain her excitement!

"It's fantastic, there are going to be sections in the paper on everything you can possibly think of, fashion, wishes, dreams, magic, shopping ... all the things that we love!" said Felicity, bouncing up and down and clapping her hands. "Fairy Godmother wants a team of fairies to put it together, to do everything from photography to reporting. She even needs one fairy to be a Fashion Editor."

Holly's eyes lit up. "How is Fairy Godmother going to choose who does what?" she asked, already imagining herself with a notebook and pen, commenting on the fairy fashions of the day.

"Well, each fairy who wants to be considered should fill in one of these," said Felicity, rummaging around her bag and producing four application forms, "and hand it in with an example of their work by the end of next week. The fairies chosen will get their efforts printed in the first ever issue."

* * *

Over the next few days the fairies could think of nothing else. Holly, who wanted to be a Christmas Tree Fairy when she graduated from the School of Nine Wishes, had already decided that nothing but the position of Fashion Editor would fulfil her truest potential.

Polly thought that she'd be most suited to Advertising Manager. She was always very organized.

Daisy didn't mind what she did as long as it was to do with flowers, but after quickly scanning the list she'd noted there wasn't a Flower Editor. Instead she'd settled on setting her sights on the position of Senior Reporter. That way she could add a flowery angle to everything she wrote about.

Poor Felicity. Her friends had chosen to apply for all the jobs she thought she'd be good at and she didn't want to ruin their chances by competing against them.

"What about Photographer?" said Holly feeling bad.

"I dropped my camera," said Felicity.

"Well, we can probably mend it," volunteered Polly.

"You'll have to find it first," said Felicity looking down at her toes. "I was flying above Little Blossoming at the time!"

"What about Art Editor then?" said Polly.

"I'm terrible at drawing," said Felicity. "Even my stick fairies look bad." Felicity opened up her homework book to show her friends her disastrous attempts.

"Don't worry," Felicity said, feeling bad about her friends' concern. "I can help you all with your articles and see if I get any ideas along the way. I think we should start with some research right now!"

Felicity, Holly, Polly and Daisy skipped off towards Sparkles, their favourite café on the corner.

* * *

When Daisy handed Felicity her article to read, two days later, it was bound in the most beautiful file covered with a delicate pattern of real flower petals.

"Wow," gasped Felicity almost too afraid to hold it.

"There's a petal from every flower in my garden," said Daisy proudly. As Felicity opened the first page, she continued, "and each page has a drawing of every leaf."

"That's beautiful," said Felicity in awe, turning the precious pages one by one. When she reached the end she looked up at Daisy, confused. "Where are the words?" she asked.

"Oh," replied Daisy, "do you think it needs words? I thought the beauty of the flowers spoke for themselves."

Not wishing to hurt her friend's feelings, Felicity agreed, "Oh, they do, they do. You couldn't put into words how lovely they are. But..." and Felicity thought carefully before she spoke, "a story about your flowers could help enhance their beauty, and make it more interesting for people to read."

"Yes, I see what you mean," said Daisy, patting the front cover of her file gently.

"Why don't we fly to Roots 'n' Shoots, to find some inspiration for a story?" suggested Felicity. And Daisy, who never needed an excuse to visit a garden centre, readily agreed.

* * *

When they got there they found it was closed. A glum-looking fairy was locking up the front gate just as they landed.

"I don't understand," said Daisy as she approached the fairy, whose badge told them her name was Sorrell. "Today's not your usual day for half-day closing."

Read the rest of

Emma Thomson's

felicity Wishes

Newspaper Nerves

to get to the bottom

of the story.

If you enjoyed this book, why not try
another of these fantastic story collections?

1 Designer Drama

2 Star Surprise

3 Clutter Clean-out

4 Newspaper Nerves

5 Enchanted Escape

6 Whispering Wishes

Sensational Secrets

Friends Forever

Happy Hobbies

Wand Wishes

Party Pickle

Dancing Dreams

13 Spooky Sleepover

14 Fashion Fiasco

15 Pink Paradise

16 Spectacular Skies

17 Dreamy Daisy

18 Perfect Polly

19 Winnie's Wonderland

20 Holly's Hideaway

21 Fairy Fun

22 Starlight Songs

23 Crowning Cure

24 Fairy Fame

25 Perfect Ponies

26 Storytelling Stars

27 Glittering Giveaways

Look out for these five special editions

Summer Sunshine

Holiday Hullabaloo

Christmas Calamity

Winter Wishes

Snowy Showdown

SEE YOUR FRIENDSHIP LETTER HERE!

Write in and tell us all about your best friend, and you could see your letter published in one of the Felicity Wishes books.

Please send in your letter, including your name and age, with a stamped self-addressed envelope to:

Felicity Wishes Friendship Competition

Hodder Children's Books, 338 Euston Road, London NW1 3BH

Australian readers should write to...
Hachette Children's Books
Level 17/207 Kent Street, Sydney, NSW 2000, Australia

New Zealand readers should write to...
Hachette Children's Books
PO Box 100-749 North Shore Mail Centre, Auckland, New Zealand

Closing date is 31st December 2007

ALL ENTRIES MUST BE SIGNED BY A PARENT OR GUARDIAN.
TO BE ELIGIBLE ENTRANTS MUST BE UNDER 13 YEARS.

For full terms and conditions visit www.felicitywishes.net/terms

Friends of Felicity

Dear felicity,

Victoria is my best friend We like each other alot We have known each other Since We Were little We always play together.

Love Georgia

WOULD YOU LIKE TO BE A FRIEND OF FELICITY?

Felicity Wishes has her very own website,
filled with lots of sparkly fairy fun and information
about Felicity Wishes and all her fairy friends.

Just visit:

www.felicitywishes.net

to find out all about
Felicity's books,
sign up to
competitions,
quizzes and
special offers.

And if you want
to show how much
you love your friends,
you can even send
them a Felicity e-card
for free. It will truly
brighten up their day!

For full terms and conditions visit www.felicitywishes.net/terms